Believe it or not, you're going on an adventure with your chemistry teacher, Morgan Swift!

You think she's really great—not like any teacher you've ever known. So when she invites you to accompany her to an exotic island republic, you jump at the chance.

But you're a little nervous. You're pursuing some very dangerous thieves, and it'll be up to you to make sure you both come back alive. You also want to impress Ms. Swift with your smarts. That way, maybe she'll take you on some other adventures.

There are many mysteries and hidden dangers in store for you. You will have many choices about which paths to take, who to challenge, and when to retreat.

Trust your instincts and think each move over very carefully.

Best of luck. You'll need it....

Morgan Swift

and the
Kidnapped Goddess

Sara Hughes

BALLANTINE BOOKS • NEW YORK

Library of Congress Catalog Card Number: 84-91790

ISBN 0-345-32367-X

Designed by Gene Siegel

Illustrated by Ann Meisel

Manufactured in the United States of America

First Edition: May 1985

MORGAN SWIFT
and the
Kidnapped Goddess

Find Your Fate™ #10

The Langford Museum of Art is a three-story red-brick building just off Main Street. Although it's not far from your house, you've probably been inside it only three or four times in your life. You leave your bike at the bike rack and take one last look at the cloudless sky. It's a balmy spring Saturday... a perfect day for being shut up in a dark, dusty museum, right? Oh, well.

You walk up the wide stone steps and stop at the information desk in the entrance hall. "Meronga?" you say to the woman behind the desk.

She nods knowingly. "Upstairs, and to your left."

Meronga is an island republic in the Indian Ocean. To celebrate their recent independence, and to demonstrate their friendship with the American people, the Merongese have sent a traveling art exhibit to the United States. At least that's what the pamphlet that the woman hands you says. And your social studies teacher assigned a visit to the exhibit as part of next week's homework. So here you are, spring Saturday or not.

You hear the exhibit before you see it, weird music that sounds like drums, rattles, and gongs. As you turn the corner upstairs, you gasp: the shadow of an enormous winged beast towers over the door!

···
Turn to page 2.

1

You catch your breath when you realize it's only a puppet—a Merongese shadow puppet, to be exact. But it's certainly scary looking, and so are the carved demon masks that line the walls. Maybe the assignment won't be so bad after all—this stuff is kind of neat.

You're inspecting a jeweled crown when you hear a voice behind you: "What's an all-American kid like you doing in a museum on a day like today?"

It's Morgan B. Swift! Ms. Swift to you and her other students. She's your science teacher, only the coolest thing to ever grace the halls of Coolidge High. She's wearing a dark purple jumpsuit and her red leather cowboy boots. She never looks like anybody else, and she always looks great.

"What do you think this thing is worth?" you ask, indicating the crown.

"Not nearly as much as *she's* worth," Ms. Swift says, pointing to a wooden statue about three feet high. It's the figure of a woman sitting cross-legged on a huge flower.

"But the crown is covered with sapphires and rubies!" you exclaim. "That statue is just wood, and pretty worm-eaten wood at that!"

. . . .

Go on to page 3.

"It's the oldest and most powerful object in Meronga," Ms. Swift says, gazing thoughtfully at the statue. "She's called the River Goddess. The Merongese believe she's a sister to the wind and waves, and can control the weather. They also believe that if she's not properly treated, she'll call down typhoons or floods."

"Where does it say that?" you ask, peering at the printed museum card stuck to the glass case.

"It doesn't," Morgan Swift tells you. "I've seen the goddess before, when I was traveling through Southeast Asia a few years ago."

It's on the tip of your tongue to ask, "Is that when you were in the monastery?" Ms. Swift's life, pre-Coolidge High, is the subject of a lot of gossip: You've heard that she used to be involved with Sting; that the silver streak running through her black hair is the result of a terrible personal tragedy; that she was once a world-class sprinter; even that she lived in a Zen monastery for a while—maybe on her trip through Southeast Asia?

But Ms. Swift keeps on talking about the goddess. "I can't imagine why the Merongese government let the statue leave the country... unless they're trying to prove that twentieth-century Meronga has no need for ancient goddesses." She pauses. "Still, they did send an escort to take care of her."

....
Turn to page 4.

Morgan Swift indicates an elderly man with a wispy white beard standing near the door.

"That skinny old guy in a skirt?" you scoff. "What can *he* do?"

"He's a high priest," Ms. Swift tells you. "And a sorcerer," she adds.

You're about to ask her if she's kidding when something diverts your attention. Three figures wearing loose robes of brilliant orange silk glide into the room. Their faces are hidden behind poison-green demon masks like those on the walls, with red bulging eyes and swollen tongues and sharp white fangs.

"Wow!" you say to Morgan Swift. "*I* know they're just people behind those masks, but they're still pretty terrifying. They're probably going to do some Merongese dances."

"Not carrying .45's," she says grimly.

That's when you notice the guns...

"Ladies and gentlemen," says one of the masked gunmen, in strangely accented English, "please to lie face down on the floor—quickly!"

Your face is on the floor in ten seconds, but you manage to whisper to Ms. Swift: "They've come to steal the crown!"

Turn to page 6.

There's the sound of breaking glass. Then, "Stay where you are for five minutes, and you won't be hurt!" another voice says...and the robbers are gone.

Ms. Swift is on her feet in half that time. As you're scrambling up she exclaims, "The goddess...they've kidnapped the River Goddess!" She sprints out of the room and down the stairs. You struggle to catch up.

Ms. Swift's old Mercedes two-seater is parked by the curb. You don't wait for an invitation. The top is down, so you vault over the door and into the passenger seat.

"Buckle your seat belt!" Ms. Swift orders. "I must have had a premonition—I spent the morning tuning her up!" She must be referring to the car, because she barely touches the gas pedal and the little black convertible shoots forward!

A dark green sedan is careening around a corner several blocks in front of you. Maybe it's the robbers! Then you notice the old priest. He's pedaling a bike furiously toward the back of the museum—and it's *your* bike!

....

If you think you should try to catch up with the green car, turn to page 29.

If you want to see where the priest is going on your bike, turn to page 49.

6

"Can you start this thing?" you ask Morgan Swift.

"No problem," she says. She sits down in the pilot's seat. She turns a key and flicks some switches. The propellers start turning...they're spinning faster...the seaplane is moving forward!

But the plane hits a large whitecap broadside. You lurch toward the windshield. You grab for something to keep yourself from falling. Unfortunately, what you grab is the control stick of the seaplane!

"Don't touch that!" Ms. Swift yells.

But you've already pulled the lever straight back. The plane's nose lifts up...the pontoons are out of the water...you're airborne!

"I'm—I'm sorry!" you stammer.

"It's okay," Morgan Swift says as she grabs the stick. "I've watched people do this lots of times. We have to keep the plane level," she adds, "or we don't have a chance."

But how do you know what *level* is when you're flying through dense black clouds, with rain pouring down, and the wind slapping you all over the place!

....

Turn to page 57.

"Water," you tell Morgan Swift. "She's a river goddess, isn't she?"

"That's exactly where we'll look," Ms. Swift says. "The Pequonset River."

She grabs a shiny purple trench coat. You pull your slicker back on and follow her down the stairs and out the back door to the garage. You climb into the passenger seat of the little black Mercedes and help her put the top up. Then the two of you are off, into the storm, and heading for the river.

Ms. Swift switches on the headlights—it's getting as dark as night out here, although it's only four in the afternoon—and tunes to an all-news station on the car radio. "Langford has never seen anything like this!" the announcer is saying excitedly. "It's like a tropical monsoon out there!"

"He doesn't know how right he is!" you mutter.

"It has rained eight inches in just two hours," he goes on. "There is widespread local flooding. Abandoned cars block many of the roads throughout the city. The office buildings downtown are losing some of their window glass to the wind—avoid that area at all costs!"

. . . .

Turn to page 40.

"Definitely the FBI—the CIA isn't allowed to operate inside the United States," Ms. Swift says. "Since the professionals seem to have everything under control, we're going home before we get wet, as Mr. Ford suggested. He's right—I shouldn't have involved you in this to begin with. Can I drop you someplace?" she asks.

After all you've heard about Morgan Swift, you certainly didn't expect her to quit! "At the museum," you answer glumly. And just when things were getting interesting!

"See you in class on Monday," Ms. Swift says as she lets you out. She waves as she drives away. Maybe she *was* worried about your safety. But you just can't believe she would give up so easily, especially since she was so concerned about the goddess herself!

You find your bike back in the rack—the old priest must have returned it. It's starting to rain, and the wind is blowing harder. You'd better get home... or should you? What about trying to find out what Mr. Ford and his friend are up to?

....

If you decide to go home, turn to page 54.
If you decide to try to find out what Mr. Ford is up to, turn to page 26.

9

The three men at the table are speaking quietly. They look as though they could be Merongese—but then why are they speaking English?

Morgan Swift pulls you back from the door and down the hall to talk. As though in answer to your unspoken question, she explains in a whisper: "There are many different dialects in Meronga—but English is the common language."

"Let's get the goddess!" you urge excitedly. "There are three of us and three of them!" You've already decided to count the old priest on your side.

"But *they* have guns," Morgan points out.

The sound of the rain outside muffles noises in the stone house pretty effectively. But suddenly the men's voices are raised...wait...did you hear them say something about a bomb?

Ms. Swift darts back to the door of the lighted room. And you're not far behind.

Turn to page 81.

10

"We have to be very careful not to jiggle the bomb," Morgan Swift says. She lays the briefcase down on its side and flicks open the catch. You're both holding your breath.

Slowly she opens it. The bomb is cradled inside on a nest of paper towels. It looks like two sticks of dynamite, a wind-up alarm clock, and a bunch of wires.

"We don't have much time," Ms. Swift tells you. "I have a feeling that when the minute hand reaches twelve, this thing is going to detonate!"

That gives you about three minutes. Should you throw the bomb out the window and let it blow up in the empty parking lot behind the museum?

Or should you and Morgan Swift try to defuse it?

··

If you think you should throw the bomb out the window, turn to page 76.

If you think you should try to defuse it, turn to page 44.

11

Your foot slips off the pontoon. You're going to slide into the swirling waters of the Pequonset! No... Morgan Swift's grip is like iron. She braces herself and pulls you back up. You're safe!

"Thanks," you mumble, your teeth chattering.

"Let's get inside" is all Ms. Swift says. You follow her into the cabin of the seaplane and pull the door closed.

Morgan Swift checks the cockpit. "Nothing!" she says, exasperated. There are seats for four passengers—the three robbers... and the kidnapped goddess? Then you find a zippered canvas bag.

"What about this?" you ask.

"Open it up," says Morgan Swift.

"Money!" you exclaim. "Stacks of fifty-dollar bills!"

Turn to page 52.

12

"We'll just think of you as my insurance," the man says as he starts the car. "Yep, you're Larry's insurance against the cops, just like *this* is Larry's insurance against an uncertain financial future...and those Merongese jerks didn't even see me take it! They were too busy clearing out with that worn-out statue."

The Merongese stole the River Goddess? But why?

Before you can think about it, Larry waves something at you in the back seat. It's soft gold, and it's been mashed pretty flat. But you recognize it immediately—it's the jeweled crown you were admiring at the museum when Ms. Swift came up to you!

Larry drives quickly through the storm-darkened streets of Langford. The rain is pouring down now, and there's a strong wind. When the car finally brakes to a stop, you see the flash of a pink neon sign through the rain-streaked back window.

....

Turn to page 43.

Morgan Swift obviously knows a lot more about this tarot business than you do. And since *her* card has to do with a house, you say, "Let's try looking for the goddess in a house."

"Hmmm." She's thinking. "Where are the most expensive houses in Langford?"

And you both answer at the same time: "Fairmont Heights!"

"But how will we know *which* house?" you wonder aloud as Morgan's black sports car scoots out of the garage and into the storm.

"At times you have to trust the psychic side of your personality," Ms. Swift tells you, "and I think this is one of those times. In other words," she adds with a grin, "I don't know."

It's raining steadily and the wind has risen to a wail. The wide, tree-lined streets of Fairmont Heights are as deserted as the rest of Langford. And the houses are set so far back on their sloping lawns that it's hard to see anything.

It's Morgan Swift who spots something that looks suspicious. She brakes to a stop across the street from an impressive fieldstone mansion. There's a FOR SALE sign in front. In fact, the house already looks empty. But there's a dim glow at one of the side windows upstairs.

· ·

Turn to page 22.

"We can't let them blow up the art museum!" you say. "It's the only museum Langford has!"

"And that exhibit contains most of the treasures of Meronga," Morgan Swift adds. "We'd better hurry!"

The two of you tear down the stairs. You're halfway to Morgan's sports car when you remember the priest.

"He can take care of himself," Morgan assures you, "and the goddess, too, for that matter."

You jump into the Mercedes and pray that the car will start after the soaking it's been getting...it does! But Ms. Swift has to drive at a maddeningly conservative speed through the flooded streets if she doesn't want to drown the motor.

So by the time you get to the museum, there's not a car in sight. You can only assume that the Merongese bombers have been here, done their dirty work, and left.

"At least there's no one around to get hurt," Morgan Swift says.

No one except you two!

....
Turn to page 25.

If the driver of the car outside is one of the robbers, he might shoot you, thinking that you're Larry. Then again, Larry might shoot you himself. You'll definitely keep quiet.

Hours pass. Larry is still sleeping. You doze yourself, waking up only when you realize that your feet are wet! Water ... there's water coming under the door!

CRA-A-ACK! The door tears off its hinges, and a great wave of water cascades into the motel room! It sweeps Larry off the bed.

"Aaagh!" he gurgles. "I can't swim!" He struggles to his feet and wades through waist-deep water to the door ... only to be swept away by the current outside! The motel must be near the Pequonset River—and the river is rising ... and rising!

···

Turn to page 87.

The robbers must not have slammed the trunk down hard enough. You drop your bike and creep up to the maroon limousine. Squatting down, you lift the trunk a fraction higher so that you can see inside. It's the River Goddess! This has to be the robbers' getaway car!

You'd better grab the goddess and get out of there! But can you manage it? She's a pretty hefty-looking lady, almost three feet tall and about two feet wide, if you include the lotus flower. Do you think you'll be able to handle her on your bike? Or do you think it would make more sense to climb into the trunk with her? Then, unknowingly, the robbers will drive you straight to their hideout. You'll slip out of the trunk as soon as the car stops—before they even get their doors open—and call the police!

If you think you should take the goddess now, turn to page 48.

If you decide to climb into the trunk, turn to page 84.

17

What's more important? The Langford museum, or making sure that a whole country isn't thrown into chaos?

"I think we'd better grab the River Goddess while we can," you whisper to Morgan Swift.

The two of you are so busy trying to decide how to manage it without getting shot that you forget about the old priest. As it turns out, he has plans of his own, and they're very straightforward—he simply opens the door and walks boldly into the room where the goddess is being held.

"Aieee!" The mustached Merongese shrieks with horror when he sees the priest. He pulls a gun out of his jacket and aims it right at the

old man. You and Morgan watch in horror, too stunned to move!

The Merongese gunman pulls the trigger ...once...twice...*three times*! You keep expecting the old man to drop, but he doesn't! He continues to walk toward the gunman. He reaches out and lightly touches the mustached Merongese's neck...it seems to paralyze him! The pistol drops to the floor with a clatter, and the gunman's body follows it down!

Then the priest approaches the goddess. He kneels and begins to pray in a high-pitched, singsong voice.

Turn to page 66.

19

"I think he's trying to throw us off the trail," you tell Ms. Swift. "Or why was he going the opposite way in such a hurry?"

There's a vacant lot in back of the museum. It's overgrown with weeds and brush. But you can just make out a faint footpath winding through it.

"I'm going to check out that path on my bike," you say. "If you'll circle around the vacant lot in your car, I'll meet you on the other side."

The sky overhead is darkening—threatening clouds are piling up over Langford. It looks as if a storm is coming. You'd better hurry—rain will wash out any clues on the path!

Turn to page 53.

Morgan Swift has to feel her way—River Road has disappeared under at least a foot of water. The little sports car shudders in the gale. And even with the windshield wipers working double time, you can't make out anything through the rain streaming down the windshield.

You roll down your window an inch or two. You get a blast of rain in your face, but at least you can see a little better. "We're coming to the yacht basin," you tell Morgan Swift.

"That's as good a place to look as any," she says. She noses the Mercedes off River Road and brakes to a stop next to a pier. The two of you climb out of the car and into the storm.

The wind almost takes your breath away. The normally placid Pequonset is foamy with whitecaps. And the yacht basin looks ... totally deserted. The weekend sailors have battened down the hatches and gone home. The boats are covered with canvas and ready to ride out the storm.

"There's nothing here," you say, discouraged.

Turn to page 42.

"What about that?" Morgan Swift asks. "The sign says 'For sale, immediate occupancy,' and yet there's a light in there somewhere. Is it worth getting soaked to take a look?" She stops the car and turns off the headlights. The two of you peer through the gloom at the field-stone mansion.

But you're the one who makes the next discovery. You see a strange shape under a huge oak tree near the corner of the house. Could it be...? A brilliant flash of lightning illuminates the neighborhood. It is! It's the old Merongese priest! His wispy beard is a white blot against the dark.

"What's *he* doing here?" you exclaim.

"I have the feeling that we've come to the right place," Morgan Swift says. "But I wonder what we should do about the priest."

Frankly, the priest kind of gives you the creeps. You don't relish the thought of walking into a pitch-dark house, possibly full of armed robbers, with an alleged *sorcerer* behind you. On the other hand, he *could* be the robbers' watchdog. And if you leave him where he is, he might warn them about you.

....

If you think you should take the priest into the house with you, turn to page 36.

If you want to leave him completely out of your investigation, turn to page 69.

As dark as the storm clouds are outside, it's ten times gloomier in here. You edge forward along a wall. Ugh! Now you've got a faceful of cobwebs. What's that scrabbling sound? You freeze. Something brushes past your leg—a rat! But there's nothing else up here.

Then you stop short at the edge of the second-floor loft. Jackpot! Below you, at the other end of a room that runs the length of the building, is a maroon limousine. One of its doors is open, and in the glow cast by the interior light, you can just make out the figures of three men. But you can't see their faces or hear what they're saying. You'll have to try to get closer!

Turn to page 70.

Morgan Swift parks the Mercedes down the block. Then the two of you race back through the storm to the museum. At the back of the building, Ms. Swift pushes open a first-floor window. You crawl inside after her—you're getting pretty good at breaking and entering!

The main lights of the museum are off, but luckily there are tiny lamps glowing low on the walls, like little night lights, every fifteen feet or so. By the glow of these lamps you make your way up the stairs to the Merongese exhibit.

Your visit this afternoon seems to have taken place days ago. But the shadow puppet looms over the door as before. And the scowling faces and bulging eyes of the wooden masks are ten times spookier in the dim light. To top it all off, there's a bomb in here somewhere!

The exhibit spreads through several rooms …and you don't know how much time you have before the bomb goes off!

"You start at the back, I'll start at the front," Morgan Swift tells you. You're the one who finds the cheap plastic briefcase, jammed between a wall and a large potted palm.

"I think this is it!" you call out in a shaky voice. You help Ms. Swift move the plant away and gingerly slide the briefcase forward....

Turn to page 11.

You ride your bike back to downtown Langford through the gathering storm. You don't find Mr. Ford in his green sedan, but you do see a long maroon limousine with tinted-glass windows. And as it streaks past, you notice something very interesting caught in one of the doors—the hem of a bright orange garment! It could be one of the robes the robbers were wearing!

You start pedaling furiously, although you don't think you have a chance in a hundred of catching the car. But luck is on your side—a large garbage truck is backing up to a downtown restaurant, and it's blocking the whole street!

You skid to a stop several yards away from the limo. You can't make out anything in its interior—the windows are just too dark. But the trunk is open!

Turn to page 17.

But wait—the limousine is slowing down. Its engine sputters and the motor dies! You can hear the men inside the car shouting at one another. Then three doors are flung open and they all tumble out to disappear into the darkness.

"Are you okay?" It's Morgan Swift, as soaked as you are. "No time to put the top of my car up," she explains with a grin. She helps you unlock your fingers from around the TV antenna and climb down off the trunk.

Your legs feel like Jell-O. "Great luck, wasn't it?" you say in a shaky voice. "The way the limo just died?"

"Luck had very little to do with it," Ms. Swift replies. She nods at someone climbing slowly out of her two-seater. It's the old priest!

"What happened to *him*?" you ask. "He looks awful!" The priest's face has a ghostly pallor and he seems almost too weak to stand.

"I've never seen or heard of anything like it," Morgan Swift says thoughtfully, "although I've read a lot about the psychic powers of great spiritual masters."

Turn to page 58.

But no—the priest is speaking softly to the beast. It raises him in the air and over its head ...the priest is sitting on its back! He seems to direct the elephant forward. It grasps the steel poles of its pen and pulls...it pulls harder...it rips the poles right out of the concrete!

Then the elephant squeezes through the opening it has made and sways majestically toward you and Morgan Swift. It reaches out its trunk. The priest wants you to hop aboard!

If you think you and Morgan Swift should ride a former rogue elephant, turn to page 68.

If you think you'll stick to Morgan's Mercedes instead, turn to page 64.

"That green car up ahead—can we catch it?" you ask.

In answer, Ms. Swift floorboards the gas pedal. At this rate, not only will you catch the green car, you'll fly right over it!

The Mercedes races up the street and squeals around the corner. "Now where?" Ms. Swift asks.

"There!" You point. "I think it just turned left at the next block!"

Luckily, downtown Langford is pretty dead on a Saturday afternoon, because the driver of the green car—and Ms. Swift, too—runs some red lights. You screech around another corner. The green car has vanished!

There are a few cars parked at the curb, but otherwise the street is completely deserted. "What about that alley, behind the diner?" you suggest.

"We'll try it," Morgan Swift says. She backs up the little Mercedes and noses it into the narrow alley...

You were right! There's the green car... but it's empty! Both of you climb out of the convertible for a closer look.

"I'd stop right there if I were you," a man's voice says from somewhere behind you. "And turn around...slowly."

The oldest trick in the book, boxing you in like this, and *you* fell for it!

....

Turn to page 41.

What if it turns out that Larry doesn't need you as "insurance" against the cops? What'll he do with you then? You're not going to hang around to find out. You're going to get out of there now—at least you'll have a fifty-fifty chance.

You stand up and move cautiously toward the door. Larry's eyes are twitching a little, but his breathing hasn't changed.

Since your hands are tied behind you, you have to back up to the doorknob. You feel for the button that locks the door...there—you've got it. But the door still won't open. Then you see that he latched the door with a chain as well. You stand on tiptoe and try to move the chain with your teeth. It's not easy to do with the gag in your mouth. But it's moving, slowly.

All you can think of is Larry on the bed behind you. Is he going to wake up?

Turn to page 38.

You have a wild bike ride through the storm, pedaling against a fierce wind, dodging falling branches, often riding through water up to your knees. When you finally knock on Morgan Swift's door, you're very relieved to hear her voice call, "It's open." She's home!

Her apartment is the whole top floor of an old Victorian mansion. You've been past the house on your bike, but you've never been inside. So as important as what you have to tell her *is*, your curiosity gets the best of you for a moment.

You pause on the threshold of a very large room and take a good look around. There's an antique oak dining table with claw feet near the arched window, and a Japanese mat rolled up against one wall—that must be where she sleeps. A square white Parsons table holds a personal computer, display screen, and printer. And there are two cats lounging on a pearl-gray couch. They barely glance at you.

But it's a picture on one of the stark white walls that jogs you, makes you remember what you came for: a smiling goddess holds a flower in one hand and a sword in the other.

"I think the River Goddess is causing this storm!" you announce as you step, dripping wet, into Morgan Swift's living room. "We *have* to find her!"

Turn to page 63.

31

It looks like a real fire to you. You'd better get out of there! Unfortunately, the door that the robbers pushed open is the nearest exit. And with the thick black smoke stinging your eyes and clouding your vision, you run right into one of the fleeing robbers!

A wiry but powerful arm encircles your neck. You can't call out to Morgan Swift as you're yanked through the door and into the rain— you can hardly breathe! The robber pulls you away from the smoking warehouse.

"I think you have something to do with this fire!" he says, his voice hissing with anger. "You have cheated the revolution of the goddess. But the U.S. government will pay quite a lot of money for the release of one of its younger citizens... money that will buy guns. So I think we will be taking you in the goddess's place... to Meronga!"

THE END

32

Even if Morgan Swift hasn't figured out that you're inside the warehouse, she wouldn't want to take a chance on burning up the goddess. You're pretty sure that in this case at least, where there's smoke, there's *no* fire.

The three men jump out of the car and tear through the door to the outside. But you stay where you are until you hear Ms. Swift call your name.

"I'm over here!" you answer. You crawl out from behind the pile of boxes.

"How did you do that?" you ask her, pointing to the smoke still billowing up near the front of the limousine.

Morgan Swift pats her big leather shoulder bag. "You'd be amazed at the things I can whip up with my handy traveling chemistry set," she says with a grin. "Even so, I can't hold a candle to this lady." Ms. Swift opens the trunk of the limousine, and there's the River Goddess, none the worse for her adventure.

THE END

"We may find something on the plane that will tell us what the guy is up to," you say. "Why don't we take a look?"

You and Morgan Swift crouch behind the pilings until the man has turned and walked up one of the newer piers. Then you circle around to the old wooden pier where the seaplane is moored.

"Be careful!" Ms. Swift warns. "A lot of this wood is rotten. Watch where you step!"

She's right—you can see straight through the pier in places, down to the water churning

below. But both of you make it to the end without a problem.

The seaplane is pitching and rocking on the whitecaps. But Morgan Swift steps off the pier onto one of the pontoons as though she does it every day. Holding on to the wing of the plane above her head, she edges down the pontoon toward the cabin. She tries the door...good! It's not locked.

She comes back for you. She takes your hand to steady you. "Wait until a wave pushes the pontoon up toward you," she says. You wait. "Now!" says Morgan Swift. You step down... you're on the pontoon... *you're slipping*!

Turn to page 12.

"I'd feel safer if we could keep an eye on the priest," you tell Morgan Swift. "Who knows where he stands in this robbery?"

"I don't think he's involved in it at all," she says. "But we'll take him inside with us."

The old priest gives you a sharp glance when you approach him under the oak tree. But he doesn't object when Ms. Swift indicates that he should come with you. The three of you slip stealthily around the empty mansion to the back door. And after a few adjustments to the lock with Morgan Swift's penknife, you're all standing inside.

"Up these stairs," Morgan says in a low voice. You stumble in the darkness. But the priest glides noiselessly up the stairs like a shadow. At the top, he leads you unerringly to the room on the second floor where you had seen the glow.

The door to the room is open just a crack. Inside, three men are sitting at a table around a kerosene lamp. And in a corner of the room is... the River Goddess!

Turn to page 10.

36

With your hands tied behind your back, it's too risky to try to get away now. You hope against hope that Morgan B. Swift will somehow turn up ... and soon!

But you sit through five wrestling matches and part of a hockey game before anything happens. Finally the headlights of a car slide past the front window of the motel room. You hear the squeak of brakes outside the door. Could it be Morgan Swift? You can't imagine how she could ever figure out where you are. And what if it's the other robbers, looking for Larry? If they've discovered that he double-crossed them by stealing the crown, they're going to be seriously angry ... and *you* could get caught in the crossfire! Of course, it's much more likely that the car outside belongs to someone just staying at the motel ... and *that* someone could help you by calling the police!

You glance at Larry on the bed—he's still asleep. Should you try to attract the attention of the driver of the car? Or not?

If you try to attract outside attention, turn to page 60.

If you think it would just be asking for trouble, turn to page 16.

37

The chain latch falls open with a metallic click. You spin around. Larry's eyes are flickering—they're open! But he looks puzzled—he doesn't remember where he is for a second.

It's just long enough—you jerk the door open behind you and slip through it before he's wide awake!

Larry's not laughing now. You hear him swear...and a bullet smacks the half-open door to the motel room. You can't believe this is happening to you! But you're outside now, running as fast as you can toward the road!

Turn to page 55.

You might as well trust the prie[st]
he knows something that will help yo[u]
the goddess quickly.

"I think we should take him where h[e wants]
to go," you tell Morgan Swift. But her Me[rce]des
convertible is a two-seater—just where is he
going to sit?

You find out all too soon—he clambers over
the door and perches like a dried-up old bird on
the edge of your knees! What if your friends see
you? You had thought it would be neat if they
saw you riding in Ms. Swift's convertible. But
not with an ancient priest in your lap!

But dark clouds are gathering over Langford, so there aren't many people standing
around to stare as you drive across town. Ms.
Swift takes a look at the sky and switches on
her car radio just in time for a news bulletin:
"Hang on, rock 'n' roll fans! There's a sto-o-orm
warning for the area. A low-pressure system is
hung up over Langford, with the possibility of
strong winds, severe thundershowers, electrical
storms, and all that good stuff!"

Turn to page 88.

Morgan Swift turns off the radio with a loud click. "I'm afraid the goddess may just be getting started," she says. "The River Goddess is honored every fall in Meronga with a week of feasting and celebration. Once, during World War Two, the festival was interrupted by a naval bombardment of the island. The goddess is an ancient power, and apparently earthly conflicts mean very little to her. At any rate, at the end of the week, an enormous tidal wave rose mysteriously in the Indian Ocean, moved with great force toward Meronga, and killed hundreds of people on the coast."

A chill runs down your spine. Langford isn't near the ocean. But it is on a river....

Morgan Swift fords a small lake in the middle of the street and turns a corner. "We'll take River Road," she tells you.

Turn to page 21.

You and Morgan Swift turn around...
slowly. Two large men in shiny suits are standing there, looking none too friendly.

"Who are you?" you blurt out nervously.

"I think *we* get to ask the questions," the older of the two men says. "But—" His eyes fall on the letters on the back of the green car. "You can call me Ford."

If he had been driving a Mitsubishi, he would have had problems, you think to yourself.

But Mr. "Ford" is talking again. "Now, who are *you*? Second, why were you tailing us?"

"I'm Morgan Swift," Ms. Swift says. "I live in Langford and teach at Coolidge High School. This is one of my students," she continues. "We thought we were following the people who just stole a priceless statue from the Museum of Art."

....
Turn to page 74.

But Morgan Swift has spotted something. At the edge of the yacht basin is a dilapidated wooden pier that no one uses any more...but someone is using it now! A large seaplane has just skied to a stop at the end of it!

"That's crazy!" Ms. Swift says. "Why land a plane here? And in this storm! Langford has an airport. I think someone's trying to stay out of sight."

As you watch, a dark-haired man climbs out of the plane. He moors it, then heads down the pier in your direction. If ever there was a suspicious character, this guy is one. His head swivels from side to side as he scans the yacht basin for signs of life. He even looks furtively over his shoulder a couple of times, though he must know there's nothing behind him except whitecaps and his own plane.

Morgan Swift pulls you out of sight behind some pilings, but not before you see that the man is wearing a shoulder holster.

Should you and Morgan try to take a look inside the seaplane? Maybe you'll discover what the man's so anxious about. Or should you keep an eye on him?

....
If you think you should check out the seaplane, turn to page 34.

If you think you should keep an eye on the man, turn to page 50.

42

"We'll stay at the motel until the storm is over," Larry mumbles to himself. "Then I'll decide what to do about the kid...." He parks the car around back, out of sight. Then he hustles you into a seedy motel room and pushes you into a chair.

"If you promise to be good," he says, shaking a finger at you jovially, "I'll untie your feet." You nod in agreement.

Then he turns on the TV set. Maybe there'll be a news bulletin about the museum robbery— or even something about your own disappearance! But Larry turns to an all-sports channel and settles down to watch the wrestling.

He takes off his jacket, making sure you see the gun he lays on the night table. He stretches out on the lumpy bed, the crown right next to him. And even before Mr. Wonderful has defeated the Iron Baron with his famous powerlock, Larry is snoring...

....

If you think you should try to get out of there while Larry is sleeping, turn to page 30.

If you take a good look at the gun and decide it would be too risky, turn to page 37.

43

You might not be able to throw the bomb far enough away to avoid damaging the museum—and maybe yourselves—very badly. You'd better try to defuse it.

"This is where that weird bomb-builder in my graduate physics seminar comes in handy," Morgan Swift says. "But it's time for you to go—I can handle this from now on." She doesn't want you to take the risk with her.

"We're supposed to be collaborating, remember? Wands, three," you say. And she can't argue with the tarot.

Ms. Swift reaches into the briefcase and studies the wires running from the clock to the explosives. "This one," she says. Biting her bottom lip, she carefully pulls the wire away. Nothing happens! "So far, so good," she says. She selects another wire... whew! Okay again.

"One more should do it," Morgan Swift says. "The blue wire, or the yellow one?"

If you choose blue, turn to page 85.
If you choose yellow, turn to page 86.

44

You hide your bike in the underbrush. Then pull your collar up against the rain and settle down behind a bush to wait for Morgan Swift. You haven't been waiting long when you see a sleek maroon limousine pull out of one of the condemned warehouses. What would a car like that be doing around here? Unless...

The limo is too far away for you to catch up with it, even on your bike. But maybe you can get a look at the license plate! You run along the edge of the hurricane fence and strain to make out the license number through the rain and gloom: "Six...two..."

"Well!" a harsh voice says right behind you. "A regular junior detective, aren't you?" You just have time to think *I've heard that voice before* when a large hand covers your mouth. "I think you'd better come with me," the voice goes on. "Since I planned the museum job for them, if *they* get caught, *I'm* liable to get caught, too. And we wouldn't want that, would we?"

Museum job! No wonder the voice sounds familiar. The last time you heard it was in the museum: "Stay where you are for five minutes..." Now you wish you *had*!

Turn to page 71.

"The second card—the Chariot—means victory," Morgan Swift goes on. "But it's followed by the Nine of Swords, a very bad card: total disaster!" She frowns and touches the last card. "Wands, three," she says. "This is a good card. It calls for collaboration, working together to end troubles.

"So, if we're working together," she says to you, "where do we look for the River Goddess?" She throws a card down in the center of the diamond. "This is Pentacles, ten—it has to do with a house, and an expensive house at that."

Then she asks you to choose a card. "Queen of Cups," she says as you lay it down. "A good card, and cups mean water.

"Well," she asks you, "is the River Goddess being held in a house? Or should we look for her near water?"

Is she serious? You just can't get used to the fact that you're having this conversation with your science teacher!

She smiles, as though she's read your mind. "Do you have a better way to decide?" she asks.

You don't—you're just glad that you and Ms. Swift are going to look for the goddess together, after all.

. . . .

So if you choose a house, turn to page 14.
If you choose water, turn to page 8.

46

Ms. Swift is one unarmed person...if these men *are* the robbers, what can she do against three guys with guns? For that matter, what can *you* do? But you're going to try and the darkness may work in your favor.

You make your voice as deep and tough as possible: "Stop!" you command. "Throw down your guns—you're surrounded!" But it doesn't work as well as it usually does in the movies.

"Quickly!" one of the men says sharply. Three car doors slam shut. The driver races the motor.

You run toward the car as fast as you can. As it backs up to angle through the open door, you hurl yourself across its wide, flat trunk!

Turn to page 73.

You're going to rescue the goddess right now—let Mr. Ford and his pal worry about tracking down the robbers! You fling open the trunk and pull out the statue. She's surprisingly heavy for someone so faded and worn.

You hear loud voices inside the limousine. It's time to beat a hasty retreat! You stand your bike up and balance the statue as best you can between your arms on the crossbar. You have to bend both of your elbows way out to the sides to accommodate the goddess. And the flat bottom of the lotus flower keeps trying to slide off the crossbar, so that the goddess's considerable weight leans first on one of your arms and then the other.

It's hard enough to keep your balance, much less steer the bike and shift gears. But you're more than a little encouraged to do so by the robbers—you almost can't believe it, but you think you hear a bullet whiz past your ear!

Turn to page 90.

48

"Look!" you shout. "There goes the priest—I bet he has something to do with all this!"

"Hang on!" Ms. Swift says. She makes a hard right. The convertible jumps the curb, bounces across part of the museum lawn, and heads for the parking lot in back.

The priest must have heard you coming. He takes a quick look at you over his shoulder ...and the bike crashes into a parked car!

He's thrown to the ground. When you and Ms. Swift screech to a stop next to him, he's lying very still.

"An old guy like this doesn't have any business on a bike!" you mutter—especially not on your new Japanese ten-speed!

Morgan Swift digs into her big leather shoulder bag and pulls out a small bottle. She opens it and holds it under the priest's nose. His eyelids start to twitch....

Turn to page 56.

"The plane's not going any farther in this storm," you say. "Let's see what that guy is up to."

"Good idea," Morgan Swift agrees.

There's a pay telephone next to a gas pump on one of the newer piers. You watch the man pick up the phone and dial. He talks for a minute or so. Then he hangs up the telephone and huddles under a canvas awning, trying to stay out of the rain.

"He's definitely waiting for someone," Ms. Swift says.

The two of you are still crouched behind the pilings. You're drenched and starting to get cold. You just hope that the man—and you and Morgan Swift—won't have to wait long.

Time passes. Your legs are cramped. Finally Ms. Swift nudges you. "Look!" she says in a low voice. "I think someone has come for him."

A long maroon limousine turns off River Road and down the lane to the yacht basin, gliding slowly through the rising water like a shiny boat. Now the man leaves the shelter of the awning and runs toward the limo.

"I have a strong feeling that this has something to do with the River Goddess," Morgan Swift says. "Get in the car, quick!"

Turn to page 82.

It's pitch black in here, but there's so much lightning that you can memorize where you're going until the next flash. The stairs end in a hall on the second floor of the empty mansion. "Now what?" you whisper to Morgan Swift.

"I think it must be this way," she says, turning down the hall to the right.

You see a sliver of light. You creep up to a door behind Morgan Swift. In the room on the other side of it are three men, all of whom look as though they could be Merongese... and in the corner is the kidnapped River Goddess!

Suddenly there's a blinding bolt of lightning and a sound like an enormous explosion over your head. The huge oak tree outside is crashing down on the house! The roof is caving in... and the droning of the priest is reaching a crescendo that you can hear over everything else. You realize too late what he was doing. He was calling down lightning to avenge the goddess!

THE END

Ms. Swift pulls a typewritten note out of the canvas bag. "'Land at Langford Yacht Basin to pick up cargo,'" she reads aloud. "'To rendezvous with the *Coral Seagull* at 2100 hours. Sutan...'"

She frowns in concentration. "Sutan, Sutan," she repeats. "Things are beginning to fall into place! Sutan is the leader of a Merongese rightist group that wants to take over the country. What better way to do it than to kidnap the River Goddess, then discredit the present government for sending her out of Meronga!"

Morgan Swift turns to you. "That's it!" she says. "And they're planning to put the goddess on a boat—the *Coral Seagull*."

Suddenly something feels different. You glance out the window. The rope mooring the seaplane has torn loose from the old wooden pier! And the storm is pushing the plane out into the Pequonset, toward the opposite bank of the river!

....

If you think you should sit tight until the wind blows you to the opposite bank of the Pequonset, turn to page 77.

If you decide to swim back now, before the plane drifts any farther from shore, turn to page 80.

If you decide to start the plane and use the propellers to bring you back to the pier, turn to page 7.

52

As you follow the path through the under-brush, you see footprints that look pretty fresh. Hey! There's one of the orange robes, thrown behind a bush! And a demon mask, too, dumped a little farther on. That old priest knew where he was going—you're sure of it!

The wind is starting to blow. You pedal faster, dodging the swaying branches growing into the path. Where could this lead? You squeeze out of the brush. And then you see it—the site for the new convention center.

A green hurricane fence surrounds the huge hole marking the beginning of the excavation for the foundation. Huddled next to it are several large warehouses, slated for demolition. Most of the two-story buildings haven't been used in years, and they look it—paint peeling in strips, broken windows, graffiti, rusty, half-rotted fire escapes.

In the middle of homey old Langford, you've found a ghost town! You don't really want to investigate any further. But that's exactly why the robbers might have chosen this area for a hideout.

Should you wait for Ms. Swift? Or should you take a look around yourself?

....

If you decide to wait for Ms. Swift, turn to page 45.

If you decide to take a look around yourself, turn to page 62.

You decide to ride your bike home and get a slicker—the storm is getting worse all the time.

Your parents are out when you get to your house. You flip on the TV before you dig through the closet for your slicker. Suddenly you hear a voice break into the regular program: "This is a weather alert!" says the announcer. "High winds, torrential rains, and perhaps even tornadoes are predicted for Langford and vicinity! There's a travelers' advisory in effect. If you can, stay indoors. Driving conditions will be extremely hazardous!"

You crawl out of the closet and stare at the screen. Now a meteorologist is talking: "I've never seen a storm of this size build up so quickly," she says. "It seems to have materialized out of absolutely fair skies."

Turn to page 75.

A bullet skips across a puddle at your feet, but the rain seems to be on your side—you make it to the highway in one piece! Now maybe you can get someone to help you. But several cars splash past without stopping. And Larry—and his gun—are gaining on you.

It's hard to run with your hands tied behind you. You stumble on a rock and pitch forward into the mud... then car headlights sweep toward you and stop.

Someone calls your name... it's Morgan Swift! She helps you up and pulls the gag out of your mouth. "There's a man somewhere behind me with a gun!" you manage to gasp.

"No," Ms. Swift reassures you, "I saw him running back toward the motel."

"He has the crown," you tell her. "He hasn't got the goddess, but he knows who does!"

"Then he may have the answers to lots of my questions," Ms. Swift says as she finishes untying your hands. "Let's go!"

Turn to page 72.

The old priest's eyes snap open. He studies your face and Morgan Swift's carefully. And he gazes so probingly into your eyes that you're sure you can feel it in the back of your head! Then he says something in a surprisingly strong, deep voice.

"That's just great!" you say. "He doesn't speak English!"

Ms. Swift shakes her head. "Unfortunately, my Merongese vocabulary is nonexistent," she says.

The priest lurches to his feet. He points away from the museum, toward the edge of town. Then he takes you and Ms. Swift by the arm and leads you to the car. "Kumari!" he repeats insistently.

"Kumari—that's one of the names of the River Goddess!" Ms. Swift says. "I think he wants us to take him to look for her in that direction."

But wait a minute. How would the priest know where the goddess is—unless he's working with the robbers? And if he *is* working with the robbers, wouldn't he try to throw you off the trail? Anyway, why was he riding your bike in the opposite direction?

....

If you think you should take the priest where he wants to go, turn to page 39.

If you decide to investigate in the opposite direction, turn to page 20.

56

You press your face against the windshield. You can't see the ground below or the sky above. But Morgan Swift's hands are steady on the controls. How can she remain so calm? You glance at her face: *her eyes are closed*!

"Are you trying to kill us?" you shout.

Ms. Swift opens her eyes briefly to look at you. "There's nothing to see out there," she says, nodding at the cloud bank surrounding the plane. "I'm relying on messages from my inner ear to keep us balanced. It's a lot like a Yoga exercise I did once—running blindfolded, learning to trust my other senses." She closes her eyes again. "Don't talk—I have to concentrate."

She doesn't see the break in the clouds. Suddenly trees and houses appear, several hundred feet below you. "We're out of the storm!" you say in disbelief.

Morgan Swift opens her eyes and switches on the plane's radio. "Now all we have to do is land this thing," she says, "and I could use some professional help with that." She flips the dial, trying to make radio contact.

"Anything you say," you gasp, firmly convinced that Morgan Swift can perform miracles.

THE END

"What do you mean?" you ask.

"I was afraid that if I tried to cut the limousine off with my car, you might be hurt. I was just hoping not to lose sight of you," Ms. Swift explains. "Then the priest closed his eyes and began to chant. He started softly, then got louder and louder. When his chanting stopped, so did the limousine. It will take him a while to get his psychic energy back."

Now she opens the trunk of the maroon car. And there, lying on an orange robe, is the River Goddess, smiling serenely.

"Why would anyone want to kidnap her?" you ask.

"This limousine has diplomatic plates," Morgan Swift says, "which usually means that it's registered to a foreign country." She reaches into the trunk to pick up a small bouquet of white carnations. "And only a Merongese would try to appease the goddess with an offering of flowers before stuffing her into a trunk."

Turn to page 78.

58

Through the sliver of open doorway, you see a figure in a dark suit glide noiselessly past the closet. Larry must sense something, because he whirls around...but his finger is too slow on the trigger. He falls forward. A curved dagger is embedded in his chest!

His killer moves to the bed and picks up the Merongese crown. Now he's gliding back toward the bathroom and the open window. Soon you'll be safe.

Unfortunately, you have a bad habit of sneezing when you're nervous. You sneeze... the closet door is flung wide open and you find yourself staring into the relentless eyes of what you're pretty sure is one of the Merongese robbers. He knows you saw him kill Larry. Now he's going to take care of you.

You read somewhere once that when you sneeze, your body is the closest it ever comes to death. Now you know it's true!

THE END

This may be your only chance to get away. You push yourself out of the chair and leap for the door. You wish you weren't gagged, so you could shout for help. But all you can do is kick the door as hard as you can.

Larry sits up with a jerk. He reaches for his gun. "Bad idea, kid," he says, leveling it at you.

Then he hears voices outside—and he seems to recognize them! Quickly, he grabs the piece of rope he used to tie your feet. He binds your knees to your chest so tightly that you can't move your legs at all. Then he stuffs you into a clothes closet. But he doesn't close the door tightly—you nudge it open a fraction with your head.

You can see Larry crouched behind the chair, facing the door to the outside. The gun is clenched in his white-knuckled fist—this guy is scared! But he's so focused on the door that he misses a tinny squeak coming from the bathroom. Someone is pushing up the bathroom window...and crawling through it!

....
Turn to page 59.

The robbers may not be far away now. But if you wait for Ms. Swift, you could lose them altogether.

You lean your bike against the hurricane fence. Ms. Swift will be sure to see it there and start looking for you. Then you try the door of the nearest warehouse. It's locked...with a brand-new padlock! Why would anyone bother to lock an abandoned building that's about to be demolished? You could be right about the robbers being in the area!

A rusty fire escape is just above your head. You jump, grab hold of the bottom rung, and pull yourself up. On the second floor of the building you push open a window. You're inside!

Turn to page 24.

But Morgan Swift is sitting cross-legged on the floor...playing cards? At a time like this?

"I agree with you absolutely about the River Goddess and this storm," she says. "And I'm *not* playing solitaire," she adds when she sees the look on your face. "This is the tarot. It often helps me to sort out my thoughts. Right now I'm hoping the cards will help me to think logically about what to do next about finding the kidnapped goddess."

Think *logically*? Wouldn't logic be more likely to reside in her personal computer than in a bunch of fortunetelling cards? A science teacher who relies on the tarot—you've heard some weird things about Morgan Swift, but this is the limit!

Turn to page 89.

"If you don't mind, I think I'll stick to the car," you tell Morgan Swift.

The two of you climb back into her two-seater and wave good-bye to the priest on the elephant. "Where are we going now?" you ask.

"Home," Ms. Swift answers. "I'm confident that the priest will take care of everything."

And he certainly does. You read about it in the paper the next day: the tracking down of the robbers by the rogue elephant, who has a nose like a bloodhound; their capture, after the elephant squashes their car like a tin can; and the recovery of the kidnapped goddess. You also read that the robbery was part of a plot by a rival political party to overthrow the present Merongese government.

You add it all to your report on Meronga for sociology class. If the next assignment is even half as interesting as this one, you can hardly wait!

THE END

You'll let Ms. Swift make her move—you just hope she has more experience with this kind of thing than *you* have.

Suddenly you see a hand—Morgan Swift's hand—hurl something through the open doorway. It hits a front tire of the limousine. Almost immediately, thick black smoke starts to billow up!

"Fire!" one of the men shouts. "The car is on fire!" You think you detect a slight foreign accent.

"Get the goddess," cries another voice.

"If the gas tank ignites, everything will blow up!" screams the first.

Fire! It finally registers in your brain! Why are you just sitting there! The old warehouse will burn like a torch—unless this is some kind of trick by Morgan Swift....

If you think it's a trick, turn to page 33.

If you're afraid that Morgan Swift has really started a fire, turn to page 32.

65

The old priest has to be wounded! He's been shot three times in the chest! But when you move closer to him prepared for the worst, you're amazed. He looks untouched!

How? The gunman was firing at him from point-blank range! Could the bullets have gone wild? The priest lifts his eyes from contemplation of the River Goddess and gazes into yours. Do you detect a slight twinkle there? Then he holds a cupped hand toward you. You hold out your hand, palm up. Into it he drops . . . the three bullets that were fired, still hot from the gun!

High priest, Morgan Swift said, and—definitely—sorcerer!

THE END

The zoo! Why has the priest directed you to the zoo? Besides, it's closed for the day and the animals are inside because of the impending storm.

The iron gate leading into the grounds is securely locked, but that doesn't stop the priest. He scales the high stone wall surrounding the zoo as easily as a mountain goat. Morgan Swift is right behind him... which leaves you no choice but to scramble over too.

The priest looks around as if to get his bearings. Then he heads straight toward the large enclosure where the elephants are kept. "Kumari!" he says to Morgan Swift.

"I remember now," Ms. Swift says thoughtfully. "The River Goddess, Kumari, has been known to take the form of an elephant."

"Well, this isn't her!" you say, forgetting your grammar. "This particular elephant is the one that tried to trample its keeper to death a few days ago. I recognize it because it has small ears."

The elephant glares through the bars at all of you. *I'm glad there's a big, strong fence between us,* you're thinking, when the old priest shinnies up a steel pole and over... into the pen with the killer elephant! The beast lowers its head and lumbers menacingly toward the priest! Its trunk snakes out... you expect to see the old man smashed to the ground any second....

Turn to page 28.

67

How many chances are you going to have to ride an elephant through the streets of Langford? The priest seems to be able to control the animal perfectly. You step into the curve in the elephant's trunk and pretty soon you're seated comfortably on its back between the old priest and Morgan Swift. As comfortable as you *can* be with rain pouring down and a high wind blowing—the storm hits before you leave the zoo.

But it's a ride you wouldn't have missed for anything. The priest directs the elephant to the art museum, where it seems to pick up a scent, just like a bloodhound. Then it thunders across Langford, trumpeting wildly.

You attract quite a parade—two police cars, several television crews, even the Langford Fire Department's emergency unit. They're all there to see the robbers, who've been holed up in a large house, try to make a getaway.

Turn to page 83.

You and Ms. Swift creep across the lawn, keeping the trunk of the oak tree between you and the priest as much as possible. As you round the corner of the house, you hear a strange noise over the patter of the rain. It's a hollow, droning sound, not loud exactly, but eerie, and it vibrates unpleasantly inside your ears. "What's that?" you whisper to Morgan Swift. But you know what it is before she answers you. It's the old priest... and you have the uneasy feeling that he's up to something.

You can't get the back door of the mansion open. But Ms. Swift makes short work of the lock with a tiny silver penknife. "Well," she says in a low voice, "shall we?"

"Do you really think the goddess is in here?" you ask, hanging back at the door.

"We'll have to trust the tarot," Ms. Swift answers.

This is breaking and entering, you're thinking as she ushers you inside. *How many years in jail will that get us?* But you don't have time to dwell on it, because Morgan Swift has already started up the back stairs.

··
Turn to page 51.

Luckily, their backs are toward you. You slip down a wooden ladder to the floor below. Then you sneak closer to the men, darting from behind one pile of empty cartons to another.

That's when you see Morgan Swift! She's outside the warehouse, peering through a broken window just beyond the maroon limousine. You wonder if she has a plan.

Oh, no! One of the men is sliding open a wide door at the side of the building. The car starts—they're going to get away! Should you try to stop them yourself? Or wait to see if Ms. Swift has something up her sleeve?

....

If you think you'd better try to stop the robbers yourself, turn to page 47.

If you think you'll wait for Morgan Swift to make her move, turn to page 65.

He must have sneaked up on you from one of the abandoned warehouses! His thick arm grabs you around the waist. "I *could* drop you down into that big hole for a while," he says, referring to the excavation. "But I'd probably strain myself getting you over the fence—I have to be careful of my back." He chuckles heartily at his little joke and you groan inwardly. He's just the sort of person you always wanted to meet...a dangerous criminal with a sense of humor!

He half-drags, half-carries you back through the underbrush to a car parked on a side street. "I've got some rope here somewhere," he mutters to himself.

The hand covering your mouth mashes you back against the car while he rummages behind the front seat with his other hand. Soon he has you neatly tied and gagged. He tosses you onto the back seat of the car. "Just like a Christmas package!" he says with a smile.

Turn to page 13.

The door to the motel room is closed and the room is quiet. Too quiet. You know Larry is inside with a gun. And it seems to you that the odds are against Morgan Swift.

But she doesn't hesitate. She rummages through her roomy leather shoulder bag and pulls out a couple of small bottles. Then she pours some liquid out of each into a test tube. *What does she have in there?* you think. *A traveling chemistry lab?*

Then she pulls off one of her red cowboy boots and uses it to smash a hole through the motel room's window. "Steel shank," she whispers. "Comes in handy sometimes." She shakes the test tube and pushes it through the window. "This ought to do it," she says.

A minute later you hear Larry shout, "What the—?!" Then he starts coughing and choking.

"Help me hold the door closed!" says Ms. Swift. She grabs the doorknob. You grab her around the waist and pull as hard as you can.

Turn to page 79.

You hang on to the V-shaped television antenna for dear life as the car bursts out of the warehouse into the storm outside!

"Morgan Swift, do something!" you mumble over and over, like a prayer.

The big maroon car skids down a wet street and around a corner. Now it's weaving from one side of the road to the other. They know you're back there, and they're trying to shake you loose!

You think there's another car behind you—Morgan Swift in her little black Mercedes?—but you're sure not going to turn around to look. Rain is pouring down in sheets—and the wetter you get, the harder it is to hang on!

Turn to page 27.

"Well, little lady," Mr. Ford answers sternly, "I suggest that you leave that to us, and stop endangering yourself—and your student here. Why don't you just get back into your car and go home before this storm breaks"—he points at the darkening sky—"and you get all wet."

Morgan Swift nods agreeably. The two of you climb back into the Mercedes, and she eases it out of the alley. Then she drives sedately down the street. "Well," is all she says.

"I'll bet that was the FBI—or maybe even the CIA—right here in Langford!" you say excitedly. "What do we do now?!"

Turn to page 9.

The meteorologist continues, "The winds are moving in a circular pattern, almost like a hurricane. But they're blowing in a *counter-*clockwise direction, the direction usually associated with typhoons in India, or the China sea..."

"Typhoons in India..." Meronga is in the Indian Ocean! And what did Ms. Swift say about the Merongese River Goddess? "If she's not properly treated, she'll call down *typhoons*."

You think of the calm face of the wooden statue. Was the smile on the lips of the River Goddess more *sinister* than serene? You're going to Morgan Swift's, right now! She's probably the only person in Langford who won't think you're crazy when you ask if the goddess is causing this storm!

....
Turn to page 31.

"I think we should throw the bomb out the window," you say to Morgan Swift.

She agrees. "If we time it just right," she says, "we should be able to explode it in the air, with minimal damage."

Very carefully, she picks up the briefcase. You pull open a window. The two of you watch the minute hand move around the face of the alarm clock...once...twice. "Now!" you shout.

Morgan Swift heaves the bomb-laden briefcase out the window as coolly as if she were at the free-throw line in a basketball game. You both hit the floor and cover your ears. KA-BLAMMM!

The museum shakes and quivers, and the glass in all the windows blows out. But you and Morgan Swift are all right, except for being momentarily deafened by the blast.

And you get your hearing back just in time to hear a voice ranting at Ms. Swift: "Just what kind of science teacher *are* you? We've checked your passport file. You've been to Meronga, there's no use denying it. And that's where you joined up with the revolutionaries. You're coming with us."

It's Mr. Ford, and he looks *very* annoyed....

THE END

"I think we should just sit tight," you say to Morgan Swift. "The wind is coming from the right direction to blow us straight across the river to the other bank." You forget what you heard on the news earlier, about the winds moving in a circular pattern. But no sooner do you move toward the opposite bank of the river than the winds shift and blow you away from it. The seaplane bobs and weaves on the agitated Pequonset, first closer to one bank, then to the other, but never close enough.

You're feeling queasy—in fact, you're feeling pretty sick. "Anything would be better than this!" you moan...but only because you've forgotten something else you heard on the newscast earlier.

Over the noise of the waves and the wind and the rain you hear a roaring sound. "What is that?" you exclaim. It's getting louder and louder.

But before Ms. Swift can answer, something lifts the seaplane into the air and twirls it like a top! The River Goddess has added something else lethal to her list of accomplishments...

"It's a tornado!" Morgan Swift shouts.

It's also...

THE END.

Morgan Swift looks at you. "Which makes me think that a rival political party in Meronga might have engineered the theft of the goddess in an attempt to topple the present government."

Psychic powers, offerings to an ancient goddess, third-world politics...in Langford?

The old priest is reverently lifting the statue out of the trunk. Moonlight shines on her calm face.

Moonlight? "What happened to the storm?" you exclaim.

"She's a sister to the winds and waves," Ms. Swift murmurs.

You look up at the clear night sky. "You don't think the River Goddess caused the storm?!" you ask incredulously.

Morgan Swift's smile is as mysterious as the statue's.

THE END

"What *was* that stuff?" you ask.

"The nearest I could come to homemade tear gas," she answers. "I'll bet you didn't know that a knowledge of chemistry could be so useful, did you?" Then, in a loud voice, she orders Larry, inside: "Throw out your gun!"

While you're waiting you ask her, "How did you ever find me?"

"I found your bike . . . and the tracks of your tennis shoes overlaid by the tracks of a large, heavy man," she explains. "The warehouses were empty, so I figured someone must have bundled you into a car to take you elsewhere. Then it was just intuition," she says thoughtfully. "Oh, and I was struck by the name of this motel."

You take a good look at the flashing neon sign: RIVER QUEEN, RIVER QUEEN, RIVER QUEEN. . . .

THE END

"There are life jackets under the seats," you tell Morgan Swift. "I think we'd better swim to shore before this plane drifts any further...or capsizes!"

Both of you take off your raincoats. You and Ms. Swift strap on the life vests and then pull the tabs to inflate them. Then you follow her through the door of the seaplane.

It's darker than ever outside, and the rain makes it almost impossible to see anything. You lose sight of Ms. Swift when you hit the water. But luckily there's a light on shore, and you churn toward it like a sinking ship toward a lighthouse.

Unluckily, along with the light goes an unfriendly voice and a gun. It's the dark-haired man from the plane, using a flashlight to lure you right to him!

"I think I'll let *you* explain to Mr. Sutan how you lost the plane for him," he says to you as you stare down the gun barrel. "You may be going for another swim soon...only this time without a jacket!"

Morgan Swift, where are you?

THE END

"But, Sutan, we have the River Goddess," a man with a thin mustache is saying. "Why destroy the museum?"

"For the publicity!" answers the man named Sutan, who seems to be in charge. "The United States government has suppressed the news of the robbery because it would make them look bad. But if we set a bomb at the museum—blow up the exhibit—soon the whole world will know. And the Merongese people will be so outraged at the loss of the goddess that they will rise up against the present government."

"Then we appear," says the third man, "and miraculously restore the River Goddess to them."

"Exactly!" says Sutan. "Do you have the explosives?"

"In the briefcase."

"Then let us go." He turns to the mustached man. "You will remain here with the statue until our return."

You and Morgan and the old priest back out of sight into the room next door as the two men hurry down the stairs.

Now...do you grab the goddess? Or should you try to do something about the bomb at the museum?

If you think you and Morgan should grab the goddess, turn to page 18.

If you think the two of you should do something about the bomb, turn to page 15.

81

Keeping low, you run back to the Mercedes and jump in. Morgan Swift starts the motor. "There's only that one narrow lane into and out of the yacht basin," she tells you. "If we can block the lane, they'll be stuck here. Then maybe we'll get a look at the driver of such a big, fancy car."

The little Mercedes moves forward. But the driver of the limo has seen you—the limo accelerates too. Both cars move faster and faster. Are you going to run right into each other?

Yes! But not just you and the limousine. From the opposite side of the yacht basin comes a third car, a medium-sized green sedan. It's going to reach the lane at the same time you do. Morgan pumps her brakes, but they're wet. She spins the steering wheel...too late... CRAAASH!

"Are you okay?" Morgan asks you. You nod yes.

Two men crawl out of the sedan. One wades toward the limousine, gun in hand. The other wades toward the Mercedes...gun in hand.

"Mr. Ford," you say.

Morgan Swift rolls down her window and smiles winningly. "Great minds think alike?" she says.

THE END

The huge beast crushes the front of the robbers' getaway car with one enormous foot, mashing the engine flat. Best of all, you find the kidnapped River Goddess, who is returned to the museum.

The Merongese government really knew what it was doing when it sent the old priest along to protect the goddess. But as an additional guarantee, the elephant from the zoo now stands guard in the museum parking lot for the duration of the exhibit.

"I guess two Kumaris are better than one," says Morgan Swift with a smile.

THE END

You don't think you can manage the goddess on your bike, and you certainly can't rescue her on foot—the robbers will catch you before you're halfway down the block! You push the trunk of the limo up just enough to squeeze inside next to the goddess. You're all set!

As soon as the truck moves out of the way, the robbers will drive you straight to their hideout. You imagine your photo on the front page of the *Langford Citizen* under a headline that says LANGFORD TEEN IS INSTRUMENTAL IN RESCUE OF INVALUABLE STATUE.

But your daydream is rudely cut short... the trunk of the car slams shut! You don't know if the robbers saw you climb inside or just noticed that the trunk was open. But they've closed it with a bang! And the River Goddess is no longer the only one who's kidnapped!

Morgan Swift, if you've ever had an intuition in your life, please have one now....

THE END

"Blue," you answer, because it's always been your lucky color. Morgan Swift nods and pulls the blue wire away. Your luck holds ... the clock stops ticking ... the bomb is defused!

"We did it!" Ms. Swift yells. You hug each other and jump up and down.

"I just have one thing to say," you tell her.

"And what's that?" Morgan asks.

"I'll never visit a museum again as long as I live," you say. "It's much too dangerous!"

THE END

"Yellow," you answer, because it just feels right.

Unfortunately it's not. It's...

THE END.

Larry got what he deserved—the revenge of the River Goddess! But what about you? How long do you think you can tread water with your hands tied behind your back?

Don't panic, you tell yourself sternly. You remember what Ms. Swift said in class about yoga: "Eliminate the distractions of the outside world."

There are plenty of them *here*, that's for sure. You close your eyes and focus on remaining calm. Very slowly, you begin to relax...and soon you're floating like a cork!

As you bob out of the motel room and into the storm outside, you have the feeling you could do this forever....

THE END

Morgan Swift turns off the radio and shakes her head, looking puzzled. "That's odd," she says. "There was no sign of a storm anywhere in the northeast on the weather channel this morning. It seems to have materialized out of nowhere."

But you're more concerned about the priest. "Where do you think he's taking us?" you ask.

"Could be the airport," she answers. "It's out this way."

The airport—of course! The robbers are going to try to escape on a plane!

But that's not it at all. You're not even halfway to the Langford airport when the old priest urges Morgan Swift to turn left. You glance up at the large sign that straddles the road: THE GLYNIS POTTER ZOO!

Turn to page 67.

However, if it means that you and she are going to do something about the robbery...You pull off your slicker and sit down next to her on the polished wood floor.

Ms. Swift laughs at your expression. "The first step toward being a good scientist is to maintain a completely open mind," she says. She shuffles the deck and lays out four cards, face down, in a diamond shape on the floor. She turns over the first. On the front is a picture of a kneeling woman pouring water out of two pitchers. There are seven stars in the sky above her. "This is the Star," Morgan Swift tells you. "It can mean theft or loss—we'll let it stand for the kidnapped goddess. But it can also mean hope, and unexpected help. Maybe that's you."

···
Turn to page 46.

The robbers are turning the limousine around. They're roaring down the street after you now! But it doesn't hurt being a Langford native. You manage to lose them in a maze of one-way streets and winding alleys. Finally you stop your bike and give the goddess a pat. You're pretty pleased with yourself—who needs Morgan Swift?

Then a dull green sedan brakes to a stop in front of you. "Look what we've got here..." It's Mr. Ford. And you can tell by the gleam in his eye that he's not going to go for your explanation. After all, the robbers in the maroon limo are nowhere in sight...so it looks as though *you've* stolen the goddess!

After Mr. Ford reads you your rights, you make the one phone call you're entitled to by law.

"Hello, Ms. Swift...it's me...."

THE END